Collect all the sparkling adventures of
The Fairies of Starshine Meadow!

The Fairies of Starshine Meadow

Daisy and the Dazzling Drama

Kate Bloom and Emma Pack

stripes

Fairy Lore

In Starshine Meadow, a grassy dell,
Shimmering fairies flutter and dwell.
Throughout the seasons they nurture and nourish,
Helping the plants and flowers to flourish.

To grant humans' wishes is the fairies' delight,
Spreading magic and happiness in day- and moonlight.
But to human beings they must remain unseen,
So says their ruler, the Dandelion Queen.

When a wish has been made the fairies must speed,
Back to the meadow to start their good deed.
There they must seek the queen's permission,
Before setting off on their wish-granting mission.

And when the queen has agreed, wait they must,
For a sprinkling of her special wish-dust.
Then off they fly to help those who call,
Spreading their magic to one and all.

When a wish is made and fairies are near,
You can be certain that they will hear.
They'll work their magic to make a dream come true,
And leave a special fairy charm just for you!

For fairies love the secret work they do,
And a fairy promise is always true.
So next time you're lonely or full of woe,
Call on the fairies of Starshine Meadow!

Taylor's Riding School

Starshine Meadow

Moonbeam Wood

← To the Next Village

The Village of
GREENTHORN

New Park

Greenthorn School

Village Green

Old Park

Wagtails Dog Sanctuary

N

W · · · · E

S

To Alon and Daniel, magical people.
KB

With special love to my 'dare to dream' dad
and my 'make it happen' mum!
EP

STRIPES PUBLISHING
An imprint of Magi Publications
1 The Coda Centre, 189 Munster Road, London SW6 6AW

A paperback original
First published in Great Britain in 2006

Characters created by Emma Pack
Text copyright © Susan Bentley, 2006
Illustrations copyright © Emma Pack, 2006

ISBN-10: 1-84715-003-9
ISBN-13: 978-1-84715-003-5

The right of Emma Pack and Susan Bentley to be identified
as the originator and author of this work respectively has
been asserted by them in accordance with the Copyright,
Designs and Patents Act, 1988.

A CIP catalogue record for this book is available from the British Library.

Printed and bound in Belgium by Proost

2 4 6 8 10 9 7 5 3 1

Chapter One

Daisy hovered in the air above Starshine Meadow, making a few final touches to her design. A moment later, she tucked her twig pen and leaf into her backpack, and with a flick of her bright yellow wings, did a quick somersault.

"Daisy? You look like a golden starburst!" called a tinkling voice.

"Rose!" Daisy smiled at her friend.

"I've been trying to catch you up since you dashed off after the Dandelion Queen's meeting!" said Rose. She had long brown hair down to her waist. Her wings were sugar pink and she wore a dress of pink rose petals.

"Sorry!" Daisy said cheerfully. "I'm just so excited about the Dandelion Queen's carnival to celebrate the oak's thousand year birthday. It's going to be wonderful – we'll all have beautiful costumes and masks. My head was buzzing with ideas. I just couldn't keep still."

"Have you got any spare ideas? I need some for my poem!" said Rose.

Daisy laughed. Rose was really good at poetry and the queen had asked her to write a special carnival poem. The two fairies linked arms and drifted on to the fence near the lane that led to Greenthorn.

With a flash of mixed blue and green light, two more fairies zoomed up from a clump of violets.

"Bluebell! Ivy!" Daisy said, delightedly. "Isn't it brilliant that there's going to be a birthday carnival?"

"Yes!" Bluebell said, drifting down on sparkling pale-blue wings. She landed beside Rose and smoothed her bluebell-petal skirts.

"I can't believe the oak's going to be one thousand years old!" Ivy said, fluttering her sparkly green wings as she hovered in the air in front of her friends. "It certainly deserves a special party."

The oak was home to the fairies' Dandelion Queen, who ruled over the fairies and gave them permission to help humans by granting their wishes. The huge tree stood in the corner of Starshine Meadow, just outside Greenthorn village.

"Will you help us make our costumes, Belle?" asked Rose.

"I'd love to!" Bluebell said. She was really good at making things and was always collecting pretty petals and scraps of sparkly stuff that human beings threw away.

"And I'll help design them if you like," said Ivy. She was good at organizing and always had brilliant ideas.

Daisy bit her lip. "Yes, thanks Ivy, but I've already thought of a design for my dress."

"Really? Have you got a picture?" Ivy said, tossing one of her long red plaits over her shoulder.

 13

Daisy took a tiny drawing out of her backpack, and the others gathered round to look.

Daisy's dress had long, tight sleeves, a fitted bodice, and a shimmering skirt with a very long train at the back. It was covered in feathers and sequins and there was a matching bird mask.

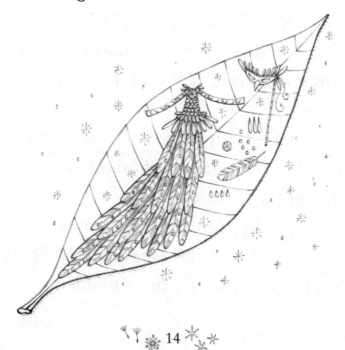

"Isn't it beautiful?" said Daisy.

The others exchanged surprised glances. "Are you sure you're going to be able to fly with such a long train?" asked Rose.

"Could I suggest a couple of tiny changes?" Ivy asked tactfully.

"No need to, thanks!" Daisy said brightly. "It's exactly how I want it."

Belle bit her lip as she studied Daisy's fussy design. "I'm going to need an awful lot of sparkly decorations. I don't think I have enough in my store box."

"We'll help you look for some," Daisy said at once. "Why don't we go to Greenthorn on a glitter and sparkle hunt? Human beings throw away lots of interesting things."

"That's a great idea!" said Ivy.

"Sounds like fun!" agreed Rose.

And with a fluttering of glittery wings, Daisy and her three friends flew into the air.

Daisy led the way high above the streets and thatched cottages of sleepy Greenthorn. Making sure they weren't seen, the fairies flew down behind a bin outside a newsagent's.

"I often find sparkly things here," Belle said.

Daisy, Rose and Ivy collected up all the sweet wrappers and scraps of foil and popped them into their bags, before setting off again.

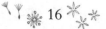

As they flew towards the school, the sound of children singing rose into the air.

"Oh, how lovely! Let's go and have a look!" said Daisy excitedly, swooping down.

"Don't go too close to the windows, Daisy. Someone might see you!" warned Rose.

It was an important fairy law that fairies must never be seen by humans. The Dandelion Queen was very unhappy with any fairy who broke this rule, even if they didn't mean to. She had to make some special magic dust to sprinkle on the human, to make them forget what they had seen.

Daisy peeped through the window and spotted a girl with brown hair pinned back at the sides with sparkly slides. She was by herself in the cloakroom and had her eyes shut and her fingers crossed.

"I wonder what she's doing!" Daisy exclaimed. "She looks as if she's wishing for something!"

Without a second thought, Daisy zoomed inside the open window.

"Daisy! Wait!" Ivy whispered.

"Oh, dear. We'd better go and keep an eye on her!" said Belle.

As Daisy made a beeline for the girl, she glimpsed Rose out of the corner of her eye making frantic hand signals. She glanced round and waved to show that she was fine, and almost flew straight into the girl!

Fluttering her wings madly, Daisy tried to swerve. But the tip of one wing brushed against the girl's sleeve, releasing a spray of yellow fairy dust.

"Oh no!" cried Ivy.

 19

The girl opened her eyes, just as Daisy disappeared inside a hat hanging on one of the coat pegs.

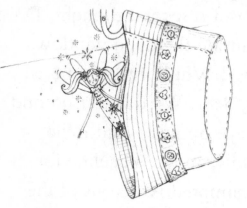

"What was that?" she cried, looking round.

Ivy, Rose and Bluebell breathed sighs of relief. "That was close!" whispered Belle, landing in the pocket of a nearby coat.

Daisy peeped out from inside the hat and saw another girl come into the cloakroom.

"Emily! There you are. Did you manage to clean off the paint?" she asked. She had curly brown hair and a friendly round face with sparkly hazel eyes.

Emily smiled. "Hi Fay. Just about. It was all over my shoe! I can't believe I'm so clumsy."

"Poor you," said Fay. "But it wasn't your fault. You only offered to help paint the scenery. Someone else left the paint pot on the floor."

"I know." Emily gave a big sigh. "Why is that whenever I offer to help, I always make a mess?"

"Maybe it's because you're always in such a hurry?" said Fay.

Emily nodded. "Mum says I should stop and think before I act."

But that's really hard to do when you're eager to help, thought Daisy, as she listened to the girls' conversation. She knew just how Emily felt.

"Anyway, why are you hiding out here?" asked Fay. "Come and have a look at the scenery, it's great."

"I'm not hiding," said Emily,

smiling. "I've just been sitting here thinking about the play. I'd love to have a bigger acting part, instead of just being in the chorus."

"You don't mind that I'm playing the Wicked Queen, do you?" Fay said, hesitantly.

"Of course not. You'll be great. I had my heart set on Snow White. I really wanted to show Miss Lewin that I could do it."

Daisy was touched by Emily's longing to impress her teacher.

"Maybe Miss Lewin needed you in the chorus," said Fay. "You're brilliant at singing. Anyway, it can be scary having a main part."

Emily gave a big sigh. "I suppose so. But I just wish…"

23

Daisy tensed, her tiny heart beating fast with excitement. She heard the faint intake of breath as Ivy, Belle and Rose all peeped out of the coat pocket and leaned forward eagerly. Something very special was about to happen.

I WISH I COULD HAVE A BIGGER PART IN THE PLAY!

Chapter Two

"I wish ... I could have a bigger part in the play," Emily said, her fingers still crossed.

The fairies watched with delight as a glittery mist, invisible to humans, appeared above Emily's head. Glowing letters formed in the mist and the wish-words hung there as clear as the spots on a foxglove.

Daisy's wings trembled with excitement. She only just stopped herself from whooshing right into view and doing a little dance of joy.

"I'm going to make your wish come true!" she whispered.

"Come on," said Fay. "We'd better go back. Miss Lewin will be wondering where we are."

As soon as the girls had left, Daisy and the others flew out.

"Congratulations!" said Ivy, giving Daisy a hug. "What a lovely wish!"

"Yes, aren't I lucky? Now I need to collect it," Daisy said, reaching into her backpack for her spider-silk net. Her face crumpled. "Oh no! I've forgotten my net!"

"Here, use mine," Bluebell offered. "We'll help you take the wish to the Dandelion Queen."

"Oh, I do hope she lets you grant it!" Rose said dreamily, as each fairy took a corner of the net and helped gather up the sparkling letters.

Then Daisy fluttered into the air and led the way back to Starshine Meadow. As soon as they flew over the fence, Daisy hurried over to her bed in the long grass. She took off her backpack and collected her wand.

Then she and her friends headed straight towards the oak tree in the corner of the meadow. It had a thick twisted trunk and enormous spreading branches. Every leaf glittered with magical fairy light, but to humans it looked just like sunlight gleaming through the branches.

Daisy heard a silvery ringing sound coming from inside the oak. "Listen! It's the Dandelion Queen's clock striking to tell everyone about the wish!"

"And look, all the fairies have gathered to see you claim it," Belle added excitedly.

Daisy saw hundreds of fairy wings glimmering amongst the oak's lower branches.

Rose, Ivy and Belle swooped
down to join their fairy friends.

"Good luck, Daisy!" Ivy called.

Feeling a bit anxious, Daisy gave
an extra big flap of her wings. She
shot forward, like a cork out of a
bottle, and landed in a heap by a
tiny arch in the trunk.

Rose, Ivy and Bluebell couldn't help giggling. Trust Daisy!

Just as Daisy scrambled to her feet, the Dandelion Queen stepped through the arch. She wore a beautiful golden petal gown and her crown was a curling dandelion bud. Her silver blonde curls streamed down her back.

"Daisy! Was it you who collected the wish?" she asked.

"Yes, Your Majesty," said Daisy, hurriedly smoothing her petal skirts. "It was made by a girl called Emily Blake. She has wished to have a bigger part in the school play."

The queen looked thoughtful. "This will be a hard wish to grant. Have all the parts been given out?"

Daisy nodded.

"Then perhaps we should help Emily to be happy with the part she has," the queen said gently. "Not everyone can have a main part I'm afraid."

"But she always gets small parts!" Daisy said, rising to Emily's defence.

"And do you think Emily is ready to cope with a larger—" the queen began.

"Yes definitely," Daisy butted in, and then blushed. "Sorry, Your Majesty. I know I don't really know Emily, but it seems to me that she always tries her best, even when she gets things wrong. And I know just how she feels! A bigger role will help her confidence."

 31

"Well Daisy, you do seem to understand Emily," the queen said with a twinkle in her eye. "If anyone can help her, I think it will be you. But remember that good magic helps everyone. So the wish may come true in ways you do not expect. There are lots of ways that Emily can have a bigger role to play, without learning lots more lines."

"Thank you. I will remember that," Daisy promised.

The Dandelion Queen smiled. "Very well, hold out your wand."

Daisy did so. The queen shook her starry wand and a fountain of glittery wish-dust whooshed towards Daisy's wand. It glittered with the tiniest little dandelion seeds.

"Use the magic wisely. Its power will start to fade after the night of the carnival in four days' time," the queen explained.

"Thank you, Your Majesty!" Daisy twirled her wand, admiring the yellow star that shimmered with its new power.

All the watching fairies waved and cried "Good luck, Daisy!" as she sped away.

Daisy thought she might burst with excitement. She couldn't wait to start making Emily's wish come true! It was going to be such fun!

"Wait for us!" Ivy, Belle and Rose caught up with Daisy as she hovered above a golden dandelion flower.

"Now I can make sure Emily gets the part she really wants. Snow White!" she told her friends.

"How are you going to do that?" asked Ivy.

"Will one of the other children have to give up their part?" asked Rose, looking worried.

Daisy's tiny face creased in a frown. "No. I wouldn't want to make any of Emily's classmates unhappy just so that Emily gets what she wants."

"Fairy law is very strict about that kind of thing," agreed Ivy.

"Perhaps there's something Emily could do, besides acting, like helping with costumes or something. That would give her a bigger role," Daisy said thoughtfully.

"That's a great idea!" said Belle.

Daisy brightened. "I'll fly over to the school in the morning and find out if there's an important job Emily can do. And now, I'm going to get on with my dress for the carnival. There's so much to do!"

"But first we should take all the glittery things we collected to Belle's," said Ivy.

"Oh yes," said Daisy, and then she frowned. "I left my backpack on my bed. I'll go and fetch it and meet you at Belle's in a minute." She dashed off clutching her wand.

The other fairies flew towards Belle's bed, beneath a tiny forest of ferns, and helped Bluebell sort out the sweet wrappers and bits of foil.

Ivy collected a pile of leaves and began sketching ideas for costumes and masks with the tip of a tiny twig. She was just passing them round when Daisy appeared.

"They're gorgeous!" said Belle.

"Our costumes are going to be wonderful!" Rose said, clapping her tiny hands with glee.

"Especially mine!" Daisy sighed, pulling her design out of her backpack. She secretly thought that Ivy's designs were a bit plain. "I've never done it before, but I'm really good at designing, aren't I? Perhaps some other fairies will want me to make their costumes too," she said, getting more and more excited.

Rose, Ivy and Bluebell looked at each other. "Why don't you wait and see how your costume turns out first?" Belle suggested.

"Maybe... But it's going to be gorgeous," Daisy said, still imagining all the compliments she was going to get at the carnival. "I'm going to love making my costume almost as much as granting Emily's wish!"

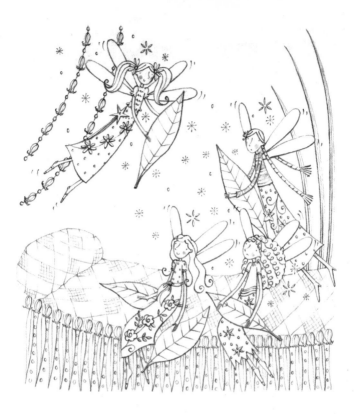

"I'm sure you will," said Belle.

"Ivy and Belle are busy with our costumes, but I've made a good start on my poem, so I could come with you to Emily's school tomorrow, if you like," Rose offered.

"Yes please! Thanks, Rose," said Daisy, beaming. Fluttering her wings, she practically danced out from under Bluebell's bed canopy. "I must go now. I've got heaps of wonderful things to think about. See you all tomorrow!"

The others stared after Daisy in amazement. Sometimes they couldn't keep up with her at all!

Chapter Three

The following morning, Daisy folded
her costume and slipped it under her
bed. She had sat up sewing until long
after moonrise.

She hurried over to meet Rose,
and they flew over to the school.
After the bell had gone and the
children were all in their classrooms,
the fairies peeped into the windows.

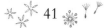

In one of the rooms a tall young woman, with fair hair and a kind face, was listening to some children practising their lines for a play.

"That must be Miss Lewin," said Daisy. She pointed to two familiar figures. "And look, there's Emily and Fay."

While everyone's back was turned, Daisy and Rose whizzed through the open window and hid on top of a cupboard. They watched as Fay and the other children acted out their scenes while Emily stood with the rest of the chorus. They all seemed happy, but Emily looked very glum.

"Oh, dear. Poor Emily," said Rose sadly. "She looks so unhappy."

"I really want to help her get a bigger part," Daisy said anxiously. "I've got to think of something."

"You will. Why don't we just watch for a while?" Rose said gently.

Daisy nodded and lay on her tummy beside Rose to peep over the edge of the cupboard.

Fay, as the Wicked Queen, had found Snow White alone in the cottage in the woods. She held out a pretend apple. "Here you are, my dear. Take this..." She stopped. "Um ... sorry. I've forgotten my lines."

"Don't worry, Fay. You're doing very well," said Miss Lewin. "A few people are finding it hard to remember them all. I think we might need a prompter, just in case."

"That's it!" Daisy clutched Rose's arm excitedly. "Being prompter would be perfect for Emily! It'll get her used to learning more lines."

"Are you sure? She'd have to learn everybody's part," Rose said, looking worried. "That's a big job."

But Daisy wasn't listening. She was thinking hard.

"Is there anyone who hasn't got a main part, who would like to be prompter?" Miss Lewin asked, looking round the class.

A few girls put up their hands, including Emily.

Daisy broke into a smile. "Brilliant. Now all I have to do is use a little fairy magic!"

45

She shook her wand gently, and whispered,

Wishes big and wishes small,
With my wand I'll grant them all.

There was a tiny golden flash and a big glowing bubble appeared. Inside the bubble, in rainbow-coloured writing, were the words, *Please choose me.*

It floated straight across the room and hovered above Emily, invisible to everyone except Miss Lewin.

Miss Lewin's eyes widened as the bubble dissolved into a tiny shower of golden dust. She blinked hard, as if she couldn't believe what she was seeing. "Emily?"

"Me, Miss? Oh, thank you!" Emily said, delightedly. "I'd love to be prompter!"

"Oh, dear. I didn't really…" Miss Lewin began, and then she looked at Emily and smiled. "Are you sure you really want to be prompter, Emily? It's an important role and you'll have to learn the play inside out."

Emily nodded. "I won't let you down, Miss Lewin," she said, looking pink with pleasure. "I'll be the perfect prompter."

Smiling, Miss Lewin handed over a spare copy of the script. "Why don't you find somewhere quiet and start getting to know the lines? We'll have another rehearsal tomorrow afternoon."

"Brilliant. The magic worked!" Daisy said. "Come on!"

Keeping out of sight, she and Rose fluttered after Emily and hid behind the fold of a nearby curtain.

As Emily flipped through the script, she started to look very worried. "I know I wanted a bigger part, but I didn't think I'd have to learn all this!" she said.

Rose frowned. "That's what I was afraid of," she whispered.

"Oh, dear," Daisy murmured in

a panic. Maybe she had been a bit
hasty. Emily looked close to tears.
"It's all right, I've got another idea,"
Daisy said.

A whoosh of invisible wish-dust
rained down on to the script.

Wish-dust, wish-dust, fly unseen,
Make the play into the sweetest dream!
When Emily's in bed, all snuggled tight,
She'll learn those lines overnight!

"Now what have you done,
Daisy?" asked Rose.

"It's brilliant! I've made the play
into a wonderful dream. Emily will
learn the whole thing in her sleep!
When Miss Lewin finds out that she's
so good at remembering lines, she'll

give her a bigger acting part in the next school play!"

"That's a clever idea! You're certainly trying really hard to make Emily's wish come true," said Rose.

"I'm really looking forward to seeing how the magic works," Daisy said. "I'll come back tomorrow afternoon to check on Emily."

"Shall we go and see how Ivy and Belle are getting on with the costumes?" Rose suggested.

Daisy nodded. She couldn't wait to tell Ivy and Belle about her clever magic!

When no one was looking, the fairies darted back through the open window, their wings flashing in the midday sun.

When Daisy and Rose arrived back at Starshine Meadow, they found Belle and Ivy wing-deep in folds of colourful spider-silk. Daisy told them the news about Emily being prompter and how she'd used her magic to help her learn the words.

"You seem to be getting on well with granting her wish," Ivy said.

"Let us know if we can do anything to help," said Belle.

"Thanks. But everything's under control," Daisy said confidently.

"Good," Belle said, smiling. "I've almost finished sewing up our gowns. How's yours coming along?"

"Fine. I should finish it by the morning," Daisy said proudly.

"Why don't you bring it over here, before you fly back over to the school? We can all try our costumes on together," said Belle.

"What a good idea!" Daisy sang out, twirling her toes as she floated in the air. "See you in the morning!"

Chapter Four

The following day, Daisy picked up her gown and sprang up out of her pretty hammock-like bed, which nestled in the long grass. When she got to Belle's, Rose and Ivy were already there, trying on their dresses. Ivy's gown was pale green with an edging of dark-green moss, sweet-wrapper stars and crystal teardrops.

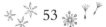

"I love it," said Ivy. "Thank you!" "Me too! Thanks, Belle," Rose said, slipping out of a pink gown with a sparkly silver overskirt trimmed with foil flowers. "I'll just wait and see Daisy's gown and then I really must write another verse of my carnival poem."

Just then Daisy drifted down, peeping over the top of an enormous armful of creamy-coloured spider-silk. Her friends gasped. Was that *all* her dress?

It took Ivy, Rose and Belle together to lift the dress over Daisy's shoulders. "It's ... er ... not quite how I imagined it," she admitted, looking down at herself.

The fitted bodice and long sleeves looked very hot and uncomfortable, while the feathery skirt hugged Daisy's legs tightly. The enormous train sprang out from the waist, making it look like she had a huge cushion tied underneath it!

Daisy tried to do an elegant twirl, but it turned into an awkward waddle and she almost tripped over. "I … um … think I'll need to practise a bit more," she said, putting on a brave face. "Could you help me take if off now, please? I can't wait any longer – I'm desperate to go and see how Emily's getting on."

"I'll come with you!" Ivy said.

As soon as Daisy and Ivy had flown off, Rose and Belle looked at each other.

"Oh, dear. Daisy's gown is a disaster," said Belle. "She'll never be able to fly in it. But I didn't want to hurt her feelings by telling her."

"I know. And that huge train will knock everyone over as she swings round in it! And she looked so upset, even though she was trying to hide it. What can we do?" said Rose worriedly.

"I've got an idea," said Belle. "But I'll need some help…"

Daisy and Ivy quickly found the school hall where the class were rehearsing. They slipped inside and hid behind a window blind.

"This afternoon we'll work on the scene where Snow White has bitten the poisoned apple," said Miss Lewin. She looked up and smiled at Emily. "Can you be ready if someone forgets their words? You'll need to keep your place in the script."

"That's all right. I know the whole play," Emily said proudly.

"All of it? How did you manage that?" Miss Lewin looked surprised.

Emily smiled. "I'm not sure. Last night I had a brilliant dream all about the play. Then this morning I knew all the words. It was just like magic!"

"That's because it *was* magic!" Daisy whispered gleefully.

"Well, let's see how you get on," said Miss Lewin, still looking puzzled. "Happy, you start." She nodded at a boy playing one of the dwarves.

"Oh, what a terrible thing has happened…" began the boy.

"Who can have done this?" Emily quickly jumped in, finishing the line.

"Emily's very good, isn't she?" Daisy whispered to Ivy, impressed by how well her magic had worked.

Ivy nodded at her friend. The magic seemed to be working!

 59

"Thank you, Emily. But you only need to prompt if someone forgets a line," said Miss Lewin.

Emily blushed. "Sorry, Miss Lewin. The words just came tumbling out."

"That's all right. Carry on, Happy," Miss Lewin said.

The children began again. But each time one of the actors began their line, Emily jumped in and finished it, and Miss Lewin had to explain it to her again.

Then Fay appeared, as the Wicked Queen. "That is the end of Snow White and…" she began.

"…she will sleep until the spell is broken by a prince," Emily shouted, unable to stop herself.

 60

"Hey! I hadn't forgotten my lines, Emily!" Fay complained.

"Sorry. I … I was just trying to help," Emily murmured, going red.

"I know, Emily," Miss Lewin said kindly. "I think you may be a bit too good at prompting. Maybe it isn't the right role for you, after all. Perhaps you could help with the costumes? It's the dress rehearsal in front of the school tomorrow."

As Emily's shoulders drooped, Daisy felt a pang of disappointment. Her idea wasn't working out quite as she'd hoped.

"All right," Emily said, reluctantly. "But it's not fair. Every time I try to help I just get into another muddle."

"Oh, dear," said Daisy sadly. "My idea hasn't worked at all. I think I'd better be more careful how I use the wish-dust next time!"

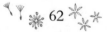

She glanced towards Emily, who
was lifting a velvet cape out of the
costume box. As the cape's folds
swished out, a pretty crown made of
leaves and paper tumbled out of the
box. It fell to the floor just as Emily
stepped backwards and she trod on it
with a muffled crunch. Her hands
flew to her face in horror. "Oh no!
Snow White's crown! I've ruined it,"

she gasped, her eyes shiny with tears.
"Now I'll have to mend it before
anyone notices and bring it back
tomorrow!"

Daisy's eyes pricked with
sympathy. "Don't worry. I'll help
you," she promised.

Chapter Five

As soon as school finished, Daisy and Ivy followed Emily home.

"My magic hasn't worked so far!" Daisy said, fluttering her wings anxiously. Time was running out and she was starting to panic.

"Don't worry. You'll think of something else," Ivy said reassuringly.

"Do you really think so?"

Ivy flew over and gave her a hug. "Yes. You always do," she said firmly.

"Perhaps I could just help Emily to be happy with her small part in the chorus, like the Dandelion Queen suggested," said Daisy.

"Maybe that would be the best thing," said Ivy.

Daisy felt a tiny bit better as they flew up and looked in the upstairs windows of Emily's house. Ivy spotted a bedroom with a pink quilt and curtains and sparkling fairy lights round the bed. "What a pretty room! It must be Emily's."

The fairies flew in through a small open window and landed on top of a bookcase.

A moment later, Emily came
into her room. She took the squashed
crown out of her school bag and
fetched some glue and newspaper.

Daisy and Ivy watched as she
attempted to repair the crown.
Before long, her hands were covered
in glue and the crown was still
looking no better.

"Oh, dear," Emily grumbled. "I'll have another try after supper." She gave the crown an anxious look and disappeared downstairs.

Daisy darted out from her hiding place, waving her wand. "Don't worry, Emily, I'll soon have it fixed for you."

"Wait a minute," said Ivy, dashing after her. "Emily hasn't finished yet. She might be able to mend the crown on her own. Why don't we come back later? If she still hasn't fixed it, you can give her a hand then. We ought to be getting back to Starshine Meadow to see how Belle's getting on with our carnival masks. She might need our help too."

Daisy nodded. "You're right. I'd forgotten all about our masks. I can't wait to see them!"

Belle's bird masks were wonderful, with bright feathers and sparkling jewels. The fairies tried them on delightedly.

"Belle's so clever. She can make anything!" Ivy said later to Daisy as they flashed up into the starry sky.

They made their way back to Emily's house and slipped in through the open bedroom window. Emily was fast asleep in bed. Daisy flew over and landed near the crown. It still looked terrible.

"Oh, dear. I'll have to help her!" she said, twirling her wand.

Wish-dust, wish-dust, let me see,
How fine and grand this crown can be!

Daisy shook her wand energetically and an extra big whoosh of wish-dust shot all over the squashed paper crown.

There was a bright golden flash, and suddenly the crown was magnificent! It glowed with gold and precious gems and it had four gleaming tiers, just like a wedding cake!

"Oh no!" Daisy groaned. "I used too much wish-dust. What am I going to do now?"

Ivy stared at the enormous crown in dismay — it was going to need some careful magic to put it right. She showed Daisy how to sprinkle tiny pinches of wish-dust, so that the crown shrank to exactly the right size. "Now we need some leaves, feathers, glitter and silver stars. Can you do that?"

Daisy nodded. Concentrating hard, she shook her wand gently.

Wish-dust, wish-dust, will you find,
The things I can picture in my mind?

With another tiny flash, a pile of leaves, feathers and stars appeared.

"That's brilliant, Daisy!" said Ivy. "You really thought about what you wanted this time."

Daisy glowed with pride as she and Ivy set to work, attaching all the glittery trimmings. By the time they finished, the first light of dawn was pushing through the curtains.

"Quick! Emily's waking up!" Daisy warned. She and Ivy quickly fluttered up high above the bed.

Emily rubbed her eyes sleepily and sat up. As she noticed the twinkling crown, her eyes widened. "Oh, it's gorgeous! But I didn't repair it like that. Who could have done it?"

"We did!" chorused Daisy and Ivy, grinning at each other.

Tired but happy, the fairies flew back to Starshine Meadow. Belle and Rose were already busy with preparations for the carnival. "It's the dress rehearsal in front of the school today," Daisy explained anxiously, "and I still haven't granted Emily's wish. Shall we go and watch? Maybe it'll help me think of something I can do?"

"I can't, I'm afraid. I still have some sewing to do," said Bluebell mysteriously.

"And I'm going to give her a hand, sorry," Ivy said. "But I'm sure you'll think of something to help Emily. Just concentrate on making her feel pleased about having a smaller part." She and Belle flew away quickly, before anyone could ask questions.

Daisy watched them go, puzzled. Belle and Ivy were acting very strangely.

"I'll come with you!" Rose said quickly. "My carnival poem's almost finished."

She took Daisy's hand and they flew off towards the school. Emily's class were in the school hall, getting ready for the dress rehearsal.

Making sure they weren't seen, they zoomed inside and hid in the scenery on the stage.

"Oh dear, this is terrible!" Miss Lewin was saying. "We can't have a play without Snow White. We may have to call it off."

Daisy and Rose exchanged puzzled looks and listened closely. The girl playing Snow White was sick with chicken pox!

Daisy suddenly saw a brilliant way of making Emily's wish come true. "Emily can play Snow White!" she said excitedly. "She knows all the words. I'm going to make sure Miss Lewin gives her a chance this time!"

"Emily's definitely going to need your help," agreed Rose, looking across at Emily, who was standing biting her lip. "She seems scared to speak up for herself."

"Don't worry, Emily!" Daisy cried eagerly, almost fluttering into view. Rose grabbed her daisy-petal skirt and just managed to pull her back before anyone spotted her.

Daisy waved her wand, and a big whoosh of invisible gold wish-dust shot towards Emily.

"Oh!" Emily bounded forward and stood right in front of the teacher. "I … I can play Snow White, Miss! I learned all the lines when I was prompter. Please, Miss Lewin. I know I can do it."

Miss Lewin looked unsure at first, but then she smiled. "All right, Emily, this is your chance to shine. Let's find Snow White's costume and get started."

"Thanks, Miss!" Emily said, her eyes shining.

Fay rushed over and gave Emily a hug. "Congratulations! You'll be brilliant!"

"The magic's worked!" said Daisy, beaming. "Emily's got her dream part!"

It was soon time for the dress rehearsal, and as the hall began to fill with children, Fay and Emily peeped round the stage curtain. Emily paled, and looked back at Fay. "I don't think I can do this in front of everybody!"

"You'll be fine. I'm nervous too," said Fay.

"I'm not nervous, I'm terrified!" Emily wailed.

Daisy gave Rose a panicky look. "Oh no, Emily's got stage fright! We need to do something."

"Don't do anything hasty," said Rose. "Emily only got scared when she saw the audience, so let's think about how you can help her."

Daisy thought hard. Suddenly, a smile spread across her face. "I've got an idea!" As the curtain went up, she shook her wand hurriedly and a sparkly mist floated over Emily like an invisible net.

"Now she'll only be able to see the first row of children, so she won't be so frightened."

Rose smiled. "Brilliant!"

Emily stood there in the invisible mist. She blinked and then her face seemed to relax. She took a big breath and stepped out confidently on to the stage.

Daisy smiled at Rose. The magic mist was working.

Emily said all her lines perfectly. She really seemed to be enjoying herself.

Daisy snapped her fingers and the magic mist dissolved, but Emily didn't seem to notice. "She's confident all by herself now!" Daisy said, grinning.

At the part when Snow White was put in a glass casket, after eating the poisoned apple, the dwarves placed the fairy crown on her head.

"Doesn't Emily look beautiful?"

Rose's lips trembled. "Yes, but this bit's so sad."

At the end of the play, Emily, Fay and the other actors took a bow.

As the audience clapped and cheered, Fay beamed at Emily. "You were fantastic!" she said. "How come you weren't nervous?"

Emily grinned. "I don't know. One minute I was scared stiff and the next I wasn't. It was just like magic!"

Daisy and Rose hugged each other happily. Emily's wish had finally come true!

Chapter Six

Moonlight silvered the branches and leaves of the oak in Starshine Meadow. It was almost time for the carnival to celebrate the oak's special birthday.

Daisy flew over to meet Ivy, Belle and Rose in their costumes. "Oh," she gasped. "You all look really beautiful!"

 83

Their delicate wispy gowns of pale blue, pink, and green twinkled with tiny points of silver. They all wore wonderful bird masks of moss, petals and leaves, with shiny streamers floating out behind them.

"Here's your costume, Daisy. We hope you like it!" Belle held up a gorgeous pale-cream gown, trimmed with flowers. The matching petal mask had sparkly feathers and silky streamers.

"But ... but that's not my gown... Mine had a tight bodice and a great big heavy train," Daisy stammered, and then a slow smile spread over her face. "This one's far, far nicer! Oh, thank you so much, all of you!"

Now she knew why they had been so secretive the other day!

Daisy quickly changed into her costume and the fairies flew towards the oak. "I don't think I'll become a dress designer after all!" Daisy said in a small voice.

Rose squeezed Daisy's hand. "No one can be good at everything."

"And we love you just as you are," Ivy said.

Hundreds of fairies were gathered beneath the oak, ready for the grand carnival parade. They all held tiny seed-head lanterns, which glowed like fireflies in the long grass.

The Dandelion Queen stepped forward. She wore a magnificent silver gown, with a tall ruff of feathery dandelion seeds, and a silvery blue dragonfly mask.

"Welcome, fairies!" she said warmly. "We are gathered here to celebrate the anniversary of the great oak. We will begin with a carnival poem."

Rose took a deep breath.

Fly the banners, light the lights,
It's carnival, a night of nights!
We fairies flutter on the wing,
Around the oak, to dance and sing.

It is the oak's one thousandth year,
So fairies all, be of good cheer!
The moon shines down,
so clear and bright,
On this, our magical carnival night!

When Rose had finished, all the fairies clapped and cheered, their wings flashing in the moonlight. The orchestra began playing and the queen led the parade round the oak's enormous twisted trunk and then up through its branches. Daisy, Ivy, Belle and Rose flew up together, holding hands.

The queen flew on to a low branch and tapped it with her wand. There was a golden flash and clusters of tiny acorns appeared. The fairies thanked the oak, before tucking into a magnificent feast.

"How delicious!" said Daisy, popping an acorn into her mouth. "I could eat these for breakfast, lunch and tea!"

"I'm glad you're enjoying the special treat, Daisy," said the Dandelion Queen. "How are you getting on with Emily's wish?"

"Very well, thank you, Your Majesty." And Daisy told her all about it.

"Well done! That was a difficult wish to grant," said the queen, smiling. "Don't forget that the wish-dust will soon lose its power."

"I won't, Your Majesty," Daisy said. There was one last thing she needed to do the next day, and her three friends were going to help her.

The sky was streaked with pink and gold by the time the last fairy lantern went out and all the fairies disappeared to their beds.

The next morning Daisy felt tense but excited as she flew towards Emily's school with Ivy, Belle and Rose. Would Emily conquer her stage fright without the magic mist to help her? When the curtain went up, Emily was looking wonderful in her Snow White costume. She faced the Wicked Queen and said her lines clearly and confidently.

"Emily's completely over her stage fright," Daisy whispered proudly. "And now she's found her confidence, she isn't making any clumsy mistakes either."

"You've done a brilliant job," said Bluebell, beaming. "Congratulations, Daisy!"

The play went without a hitch. At the end, everyone took a bow and then Miss Lewin made a special announcement to the audience of parents and friends. "Emily Blake took over the part of Snow White at the very last moment. I think she deserves an extra clap!"

"Hurrah for Emily!" Daisy shouted impulsively, but luckily no one had heard in all the other noise.

Ivy, Belle and Rose grinned.

As everyone clapped, Emily's eyes shone with happiness. There was just one more thing for Daisy to do.

Rose found a feather which had fallen from the crown and, all together, the fairies whispered,

Fairies all will make a charm,
To bring good luck and do no harm!

Daisy waved her wand. There was a gold flash and a final burst of sparkly wish-dust shot out and sprinkled over the feather. The fairies blew gently, and tiny writing appeared in shimmering gold letters.

Fairy light of pinks and blues
Brings a promise just for you.
If you're sad or if you're worried,
Make a wish but don't be hurried.
For fairies who are gathered near,
Are always close, so they can hear.

When no one was watching, the fairies flew out and tucked the feather into Snow White's crown, which lay at the side of the stage.

They had only just hidden themselves again, when Emily rushed over and picked it up.

"What's this?" she gasped, spotting the twinkling feather. Her face shone with wonder as she ran her fingers over the glittering letters.

The instant she had finished reading the poem, the feather shot

out of her hand and dissolved into a shower of golden dust.

"Maybe a fairy really did hear my wish!" Emily said. She lowered her voice to a whisper. "If you can hear me – thank you very much!"

Daisy's tiny face filled with happiness. "You're welcome!"

Belle and the Magic Makeover

"I wish this park could be as good as new."

Fiona's park is full of litter and needs a makeover
fast! Can Belle work her magic and help make
Fiona's wish come true…?

Rose and the Perfect Pet

"I wish I could somehow have a dog."

Neema wants a dog more than anything, but her
mum and dad have said no. Can Rose make
Neema's wish come true without upsetting
her parents…?